For our dolphins—Ana, Gabri, Kobi, Leo, and Zoë—whose smiles
bring so much joy to our lives and the world around them.
—SA & AB

To my daughter, Iside, for teaching me to keep smiling.
—CR

Published by Little Pickle Press, an imprint of Sourcebooks Jabberwocky
P.O. Box 4410, Naperville, Illinois 60567–4410 • (630) 961-3900 • sourcebookskids.com
Library of Congress Cataloging-in-Publication Data is on file with the publisher.
Source of Production: Leo Paper, Heshan City, Guangdong Province, China
Date of Production: October 2019 • Run Number: 5016400
Printed and bound in China.
LEO 10 9 8 7 6 5 4 3 2 1

How to Make a
Shark Smile

How a Positive Mindset
Spreads Happiness

Words by bestselling authors Shawn Achor and Amy Blankson
Pictures by Claudia Ranucci

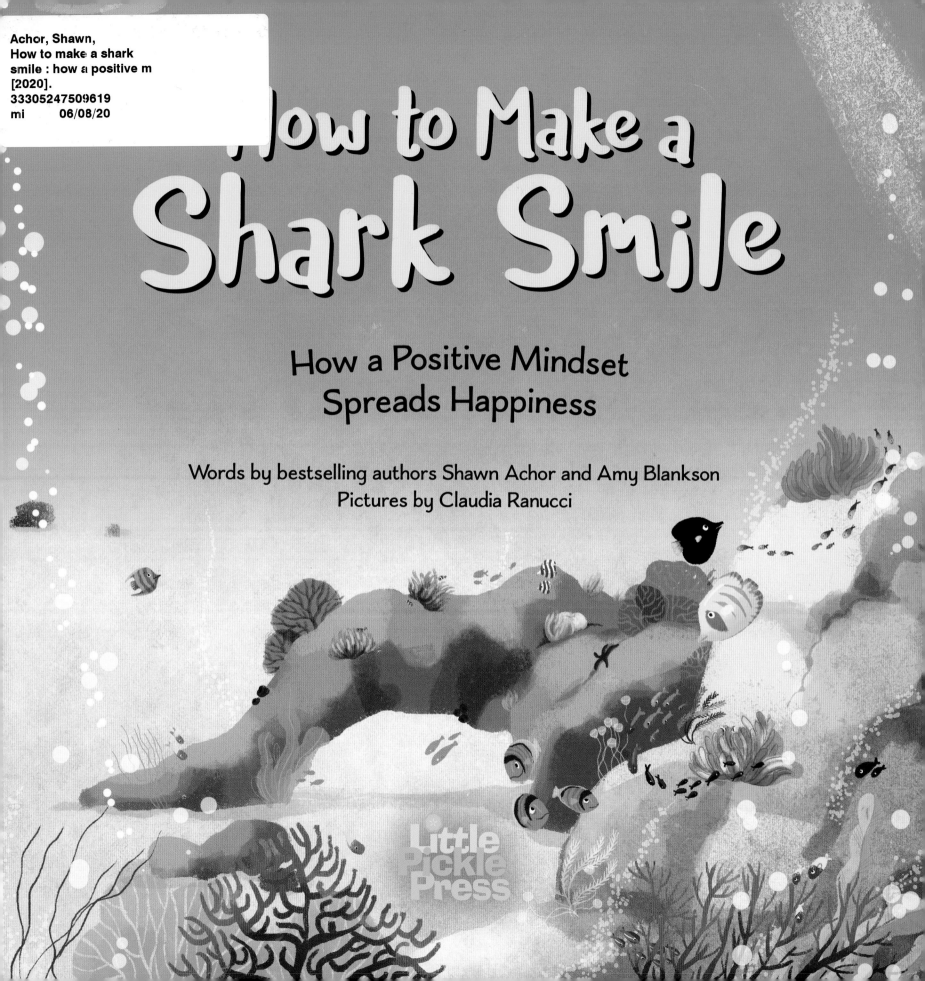

Little
Pickle
Press

It was Ripple's first day in a new aquarium.
She was excited to make some new friends!

Ripple looked around for someone to play with. But the water was still and quiet.

She saw electric eels
with no zing.

The neon fish had no glow.

And even the seahorses weren't horsing around.
All the animals look scared and unhappy.

Ripple saw a blowfish nearby and decided to ask why everyone was so sad.
"Hello there," she said with a smile.
The blowfish began yelling, "Shark alert! Shark alert!" and puffed up like a balloon.
Ripple realized the blowfish must think that *she* was the shark!

Laughing, Ripple swam toward the blowfish and explained, "I'm not a shark! I'm a dolphin. My name is Ripple. What's your name?"

"Whew!" the blowfish sighed. "I'm Bob. I thought you were Snark!"

"Who?" Ripple asked.

"He's the biggest, meanest shark you've ever seen. I've heard he's eaten entire tanks of fish when he wasn't even hungry!"

"Oh, yikes! Is that why everyone is so scared?" Ripple paused for a moment and then said, "I won't let a shark steal my happiness. Come on, let's play!"

"What if Snark sees us? You're not scared because you're big, fast, and smart. But I'm just a bite-size fish trying to make it in the world."

"Oh, my friend, it's not my size or speed that makes me powerful or brave. It's my mindset! I believe that my behavior matters. And today I choose to be happy."

Bob was confused. *How can you choose to be happy?*

"Can I show you how it works in a game?" Ripple asked.

"Okay," Bob agreed. "But only if Snark doesn't see us playing."

"Actually, I want you to play the game *with* Snark! But I'll show you first."

A game with Snark!?
Bob thought.

"All you have to do is look at my face for seven seconds and try not to smile. OK?"

Bob nodded and filled up his body with water to prepare himself.
At first, it was easy for him not to smile.

But then Ripple flashed him a big smile and started to blow bubbles. Bob burst out laughing.

"AHA! You see?" Ripple said. "Happiness is hard to resist. When you see someone else smile, it makes you want to smile too. I call it the Ripple Effect. When you believe that you can make a difference, you can change the world around you."

"That's amazing!" Bob said. "I've got to try this game out with my other friends."

He swam over to the seahorses to try out his new trick. Then the seahorses started to teach the neon fish.

Pretty soon, the whole tank was smiling and laughing.

That is…until Snark appeared. "What is all this laughing about?" Snark hissed, flashing his sharp, pointy teeth. The other fish froze in fear.

"We're playing!" Ripple said with a smile. "Do you want to play too?"
Snark frowned with disbelief. "Sharks can't play. We're born to be mean."

"You can play! Happiness is a state of mind—it's a choice that's up to you," Ripple answered. "How about we make a deal? If we can make you smile, we all get to play to our hearts' content. If we can't, then everyone in the tank will stop having fun…forever. What do you think?"

A murmur spread across the crowd. Snark sneered with confidence and nodded. "It's a deal."

Ripple winked at Bob, and the blowfish nodded back.

"Okay," Bob explained, "all you have to do is look into my eyes for seven seconds. I'll try to get you to smile and we'll see if you can keep a straight face. If you can't, I win."

Bob swam up to Snark and looked him in the eyes. He was tempted to run away, but he realized this was his chance to make a difference!

Without a moment to lose, Bob burst into the biggest, cheesiest, happiest grin you have ever seen.

At first, Snark was confused by Bob smiling at him—no one ever smiled at sharks! But after a few seconds, he started to feel very uncomfortable. It felt like a bubble inside him was trying to rise to the surface.

He tried everything to stop it.

He squinted his eyes shut,

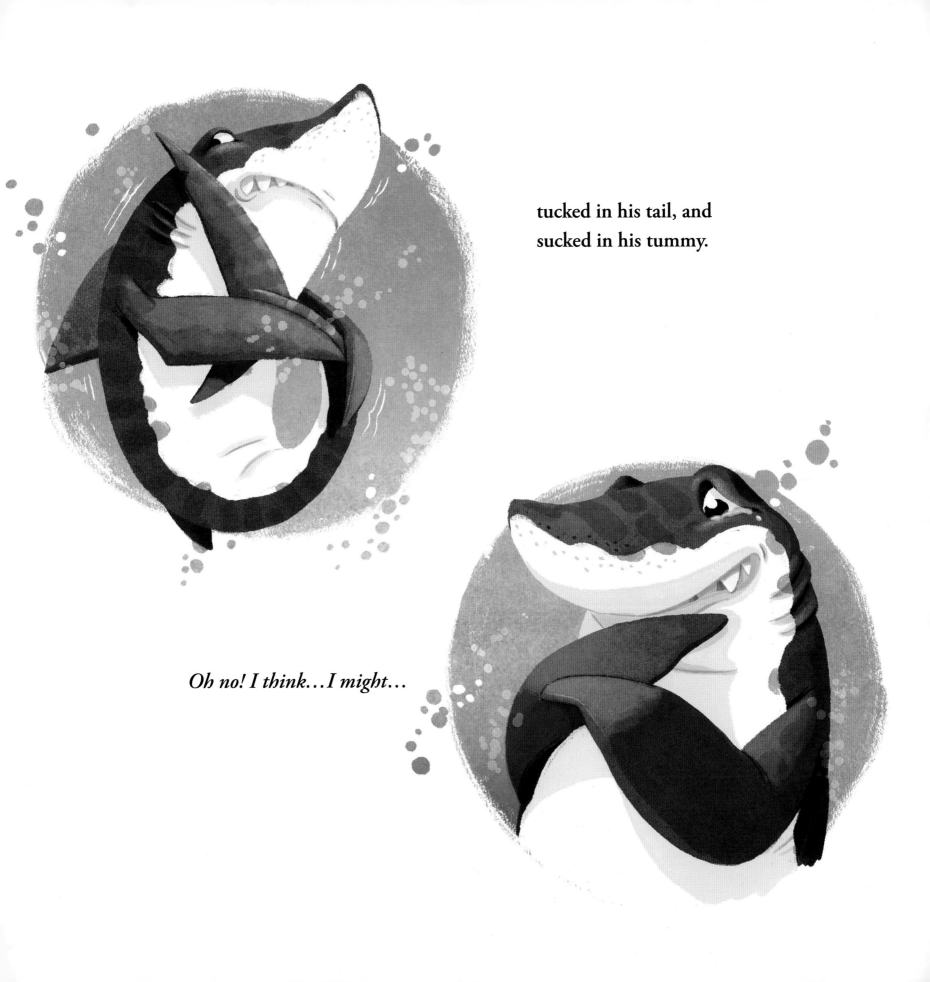

tucked in his tail, and
sucked in his tummy.

Oh no! I think…I might…

Suddenly, an explosion of bubbles escaped his mouth. He made an odd sound like a hiccup and a sneeze combined. Surprised, Snark started laughing.

Snark laughed so hard that the entire tank broke out in giggles.

Outside the tank, tourists started to snap pictures and smile as they watched. A shark, a blowfish, and a dolphin laughing and playing together? This would go down in the history books!

When Snark finally caught his breath from laughing,
he put out his fin to give Bob a high five.

"Wow, that was amazing!" Snark said. "I guess sharks *can* have fun, if they choose!"

Ripple's effect on the tank could be felt from that day on. By making a choice to be positive, she spread happiness to others and made it easier for them to choose happiness too!

CAN YOU MAKE A SHARK SMILE TODAY?

Try this experiment: Have a friend, parent, or teacher try to keep their face straight for seven seconds. Then flash them a big, goofy smile and see if you can get them to smile too! Most people can't resist.

Ripple shows us that it's possible to spread happiness to those around us. You don't have to be a grown-up or have a fancy title—each of us has the power to make a difference. But it all starts with our mindset. Mind-*what*? That's right, mindset. Mindset is simply the way that we think, and it turns out we have a CHOICE about how we think. Ripple chose to have a positive attitude and was able to spread her mindset to the rest of the aquarium. You can be just like Ripple!

To help you develop a happiness mindset, here are some happiness exercises.
Try to fit one (or all) into your daily routine—you won't be able to help but be happier!

- Watch Your Breath: When you're feeling anxious or down, pause and take a few deep breaths in and out. By paying attention to your body and focusing on your breath, your brain will begin to settle and you will start to feel happier and more in control.

- Track Your Gratitudes: Each day write down three things that you are grateful for. Writing down gratitudes teaches your brain to look for the good in life and not get stuck on the bad. Try not to repeat any entries because you want to train your brain to think differently. You may have to get creative! Also, challenge your whole family to join you—it multiplies the happiness (and makes sure you don't forget).

- **Choose to Be Kind:** Did you know that when you choose to do something kind for someone else, it instantly puts you in a good mood? Try doing a random act of kindnesss—say something nice to someone around you, make a drawing for a friend, or just help out around your house or school. Acts of kindness bring joy to others and make you happier too!

- **Get Moving:** Do some jumping jacks, run around your backyard, have a dance party! Walk, bike, stretch, jump—getting in some exercise every day will keep your mood sunny!

- **Look Forward to Good Things:** What's something good that might be happening later today or this week? Maybe your best friend is coming over for dinner or you get to play sports. Or maybe you are excited about a new movie coming out or a trip coming up. Thinking about good things coming in the future can help brighten your mood and get you focusing on happy thoughts again.

- **Do Something You Love Doing:** We all have talents and strengths, and we all have special interests and things that excite us. When we have opportunities to focus on these things, they remind us that we are unique, special, and valuable—and in return, we're happier!

- **Keep a Journal:** At the end of each day, think about the most meaningful moment in your day. Write down everything you can remember about that moment—who you were with, what you were doing, and why that moment was meaningful. By writing about this moment, your brain relives the best part of your day and you get double the happiness!

For more ideas on bringing the science of happiness to life, visit MakeaSharkSmile.com.